*Yarrow Paisley*

# MENDICANT CITY

Yarrow Paisley was born shortly after the American Bicentennial. He graduated from Bard College with a BA in Literature and has since worked in various professions, including bookseller, photographer, lab grunt, gambler, clipboard canvasser, factory drudge, and USPS letter carrier. His fiction has appeared in a variety of journals and anthologies, including *Strange Tales V* (Tartarus Press), *Dadaoism* (Chômu Press), and *Marked to Die* (Snuggly Books). He lives in the Pioneer Valley of Western Massachusetts.

# yarrow paisley
# mendicant city

Snuggly Slim no. 6

THIS IS A SNUGGLY BOOK



Cover art: Logan Zander Smith

ISBN: 978-1-943813-17-9

**Acknowledgements**

"Genius & Claudette" appeared in *Museum Life* (2013). "Rumour's Run" appeared in *3rd bed* (2003) and *Van Gogh's Ear Anthology* (2014). "The Vain Vein" appeared in *Denver Syntax* (2009). "I Curse the Curs!" appeared in *Untoward* (2011). "Bone Hotel" appeared in *Twelve Stories* (2011). "A Universal Sensation" appeared in *L'Allure des Mots* (2013). "The Pain Painter" appeared in *Abjective* (2010). "In That Country" appeared in *Kerouac's Dog* (2012). "What Breathes Down There?" appeared in *Glass Eye Chandelier* (LucidPlay Publishing, 2013).

# Contents

mendicant city

# I Am the City

DO not forgive me, Man, for *I have sinned.*

I am all of the millions, and I am myself one of the millions. They crowd within me, the people, and rampage among my tissues. Their frenzy is perpetual. Each one of them weeps, and brings into my body his or her own pain, and the pain of one becomes my pain, and becomes the pain of millions. It is an awesome responsibility, and I bear it because I love them. I would not do so, otherwise.

Yet . . . *I have sinned.*

I love them, but their pain is great. I confess, I have thought of myself. I have ordained myself: "I." I have imagined myself an entity not of *them*, but of something *altogether new.* But I have not set myself *higher*, I tell you, but *apart. I love them*, more than I do this voice. I love them as *I know them*, more than I do this voice. Yet I am coming to know my voice, and I am coming to love it too.

And *I have sinned*, and this is my sin:

# Genius & Claudette

EVERY day, he requires me in his studio. I undress, and he informs me carefully exactly how I should pose; and if I should waver just a bit, he explodes with fury, but this is not his fault. He is a genius. Genius commands him. He is a gentle soul otherwise.

"Claudette," he told me that first time, his voice wet and nervous, "your body is the Eden of my art. I must travel there to find my paradise. I need you." I had nothing better to do. The pay was more than adequate. I assented, and he gave me directions to his studio. That was five years ago. I have posed for him every day since, excluding several few holidays at his insistence.

He is not much to look at, but then, he is not the model, is he? I am, and I am beautiful. This is not vanity, but commodity: my beauty is my traffic. He pays me well enough. It is my duty.

He speaks sometimes while he paints. Not often, but over the years the words have accumulated. At first, I ignored them as eccentricities. Gradually, I came to look forward to his strange ejaculations; in some small degree, they dispelled the monotony of the sessions. I began a collection.

> *O, here is that ecstasy I sought! But no. . . . No. It is bitter.*

That was the first one I jotted down. Something about it compelled me to purchase a notebook and pen, to begin my collection. (Bear in mind, by the way, that my inadequate memory sometimes forces me to paraphrase.)

*Something in concern of penguins. Penguins are the key.*

*You are rambunctious, Red. You will get away from me if I am not careful. There now—there is your corral.*

*There is a mountain in this plain [plane?], somewhere a mountain. . . . [Some time later:] The peak, it is rising. . . . There. There. There. O yes, the mountain o'erlooms the huts! There. . . . The huts so small. . . . But the sky has gone grey, and her body dwindles with the light. Claudette, your finger! Move it back! The sky is changing!*

(He can be harsh sometimes.)

*Love moves through this brush. I am painting love. Love is neither man nor woman. Love is this canvas, having been touched by the brush.*

*It is a nation. Here are her boundaries. Here are her territories. She expands and contracts according as her interests fortify and wane. She exploits her resources with care, for they are finite. Others covet what she possesses, and she must lord jealously over her lands. Yet, mayhap, Treaty?*

*Down, Yellow, down! Seek further downward. Do
not attempt to thwart me!*

*Ten thousand million degrees round the point must this
rotation achieve. The point is in the selectest spot, I have
chosen it with precision such as no man alive may attain
to its placement, and here, in these thick oil swabs, I will
achieve the degrees!*

*O! O!*

*And here, here is nomenclature of the visual dimen-
sion. Who may converse according to these signs? Who
may know the mysteries I am inserting here? Am I the
only of this kind? Am I the Sole Sibling in this mad
Family?*

This one is my favorite:

*Never was there beauty before there was Claudette.*

And here is one of greater duration, more of a so-
liloquy than an outburst. It was a rare moment. He even
paused in his painting and stepped to the window, gazing
out into the rainy street as he delivered the speech:

*I have been into that other world. I have scavenged there,
brought back wonders. I have seen God's face,—and yet
for all its shining, my eyes were not blinded. Here—
here are the colors. I know them intimately. My
congress with them is such that the subtlest gradients*

*across my canvas are to me vivid and obvious. Where other men perceive a monochrome, I perceive a rainbow. And yet, Claudette* [I was quite startled to hear my name], *where are my wings? I know Beauty* [he gestured to his easel], *but I do not know beauty* [he looked directly at me]. *I will die, like other men. I am mortal, and acquiescent to this. But I had hoped . . . in my youth . . . I had hoped . . .* [Here he lapsed into silence, poking the handle of his brush deep into his beard, as I have seen him do in instances of contemplation. Some moments later, he resumed:] *I am a man. Against my will, I am only a man. And here you are, Claudette, a woman, beautiful as none on Earth before you have been. Is it against your will?* [I took this rhetorically.] *Is it* your *doing that a man like me would give all he owned to possess you? Is it* your *doing that no man may ever possess you?* Your colors shine, *Claudette! I have attempted to mark you in Beauty, and I know I never shall. I have at my disposal only the instruments of God's design, and these are insufficient. You are beautiful and you will die; whereas this painting is immortal and its colors next to yours are mud. I look at you, and am blinded, blinded even unto the grave. I love you, Claudette.*

I take no account of such statements as that last. The man is a genius, subject to his eccentricities. He is in love with his painting, and only ever his painting.

I must admit, I enjoy posing for him. He is an exacting master, but I am accustomed to his rigors. My skill has increased since I have come into his employ, so that I can hold a pose now almost indefinitely. An artist of his caliber condones no frequent breaks on the model's part. I need rest only once in an entire sixteen-hour session, and even that half-hour he grants grudgingly. I am ravenously hungry when, at the end of the day, the candle sputtering in the last of its wax rings the tocsin of an end to painting. He is hungry too. Often, we eat together; there is a fine restaurant just around the corner from his studio. Meats and vegetables, and delicious gravies: he is well-off, he takes care of the bill. In the beginning, he ate dry things, and cold things, but I gave him immediately to understand that I prefer a *cooked* meal. He shrugged, and smiled, and said, "Whatever you prefer, my dear. I will eat it with you, and prefer it too." When not at his genius, he really is quite gentle.

# My Birth's Revenge

I WAS born of an incest between my mother and her son. My father died conceiving me, crushed under our mother's body as she rutted him. Her ecstasy occurred at the instant of his last asphyxiated gasp for life. She recounted the tale to me mirthfully throughout my childhood.

I left home at the age of eight. I wandered our nation's roads and made my bed in the garbage dumps.

It is not difficult for a young boy to hitch. Not even thumbs are required, only buns. The cars pant and huff as they rush past, and finally one of them cannot resist the luscious temptation, and slows, and waits. The young boy trots to meet it. A mechanic whir sounds, a window rides down. A body inside leans at the hip to clutch the boy with its clutching eyes. The door swings wide, the boy crawls inside, clumsily drawing the door shut behind him.

Finally, I reached the sea. The waves raced toward me; then, exhausted, receded defeated. But they kept trying. I'll give them that. Ultimately, the sea had no strength to claim me. I remained dry. The sea howled its despair to the moon. The moon licked its lips, hushed the tempest with its lambent embrace. The moon smiled like a mother but could not seduce me.

I rode in a truckbed to the site of the World's Fair. The sun blazed at the pinnacle of the Tower of Beauty, which was the Fair's hence-eternal monument. I reviled the sun for its hypocrisy in reducing itself to a mere trophy for the pygmied masses of men to cluck over. Even the sun had betrayed me!

I knew there was no recourse for me. There was no place I could hide on this Earth, in life or in death. I would always be at the mercy of energy. My indivisibles would never divide. The atom has always rejected my pleas, no matter the passion with which I deliver them.

What monster conceived me? My own brother. The demon connived to "fall victim" to my mother's innocent lust. I cannot forgive him that, even though he was of my flesh. Somewhere his energy persists, and I curse it. I would like to thrust my hard boy's cock into its virgin anus. This would be my birth's revenge.

# Rumour's Run

I RAN.

Towns took me in, but never for more than a few days. The townspeople were generous, but they did not wish to harbor a fugitive from the horseman. I did not blame them. I would have done the same, *in their position*.

I saw slim girls swimming in a shallow pond. Their bright eyes, their angling backs, the archery of their bodies: the scene drew my interest. Their throats emitted shrieks: I thought, *Pain!* But no, this was not pain. The water grew red. I thought, *Save them! Help them!* But they refused my assistance even before I offered it, *refused* without even knowing of my presence in the hedges. I stalked off, and they never saw me. The horseman was quick on my trail. I heard their screams behind me, and I thought, *Joy!* I did not turn to confirm this; in retrospect I regret the lapse.

I thought, *Apocalypse has come!* For some of the cities were in ruins. But then there were the thriving metropoli to thwart my theory. Yet——I *knew* Armageddon was *biding*,—in the despairless throngs, in the grim mouths of the streets through which throbbed the tired traffic tongues, in the rust squeals of the mayors' bones, in the satisfaction of the winos, in the writhing rainbow skies of twilight. The cities *slept by day*, and at night arose in hideous bodies, syphilitic, asthmatic, languid and shuddering weak, but strong enough to stroke their organs, to climax in the dawn, to fade (gratefully) into that fitful sunlit slumber. The cities did not take me in, nor expel me. But they answered the horseman's queries as to my whereabouts, to the best of their knowledge: they saw no profit in protecting me, and possibly feared the horseman's reprisal should they be less than honest. I did not blame them. I would have done the same, *in their position.*

I heard the hunt crashing through the brambles of the wood. I hid. Near me was a bleeding boy. He gasped and shook, and the galloping blasts of firearms in the distance shocked and swept him swooning. I took the boy up in my arms, and noted he was light. I carried him all night through the gaps between the trees, from gap to gap, *traversing the gaps.* The boy slept peacefully in my arms, and his blood stained my shirt, but it was old blood, for the bleeding had stopped. I licked his wound, confident he would not wake to my tongue. I found I enjoyed the taste of his blood, so I probed at the wound with the tip of my tongue until its seam burst and new blood seeped out. This invigorated me, and I *traversed the gaps* at a far greater pace. But the horseman was quick on my trail, and I dropped the boy. The boy still slept on the ground where he landed. I found a way out of the wood, and behind me I heard the horseman and the boy. I should not have dropped him. He may have had a sister, as I have a sister.

I stumbled into a vast network of caverns in which dwelt men with slight bodies, attenuated limbs, milky flesh. They fed me, and medicated and clothed me. Their bodies were so soft. I slept on them; they gladly played my mattress: *it was their pleasure.* As I slept, the softness of their bodies softened; a cool, liquescent soma flowed into my breath. My body filled with inhalations that weighed me to the rock and would not let me rise. When I awoke, perspiring and thirsty, I fell asleep again. When I awoke a second time, merely thirsty, I dipped my tongue in the puddle that had formed around me. I slept again, and rose refreshed. But I did not pause to enjoy my state; for I could hear the horseman in the tunnels now, and already my good health pursued the wane.

A mountain loomed in my way, and I began to climb. I did not stop to rest, not once, but *plummeted inversely* with the very *gravity* of the horseman, which sought to drag me back down the mountainside. When I reached the top, I discovered a cabin nestled in the rocks. A blind hermit lived there. He took me in. He did not demand I leave. I told him of the horseman, for I am honest, although fugitive. He laughed. He told me, *I know of this horseman. I too have been in his clutches. I too have escaped.* Suddenly, I felt uneasy. I told the hermit I could not stay. He told me, *You will be safe here. The horseman will never reach here.* I told the hermit I must leave. He grabbed at my arm, but I shook him off. He lunged at me, but since he was blind it was easy to evade him. I heard his howls for hours as I stumbled down the other side of the moun- tain. I did not blame him. I would have done the same, *in his position.*

I thought, *Apocalypse has come!* For before me, on a plain, armies were assembling for war. Flames serrated the horizon, and the sky was a spectrum from crimson to black. I walked through the encampments, and no one noticed me. A tearful woman performed a tracheatomy on a convulsing toddler. A naked boy beat a drum with his erect member before an audience of haggard men. An amputated soldier practiced swordplay. A priest tore his vestments on a protruding nail and cursed. Some of the tents were squirming. A dead whore lay in the street, and a crouching girl attempted to wrench some rings from the swollen fingers. The armies could be seen out on the field, beginning the engagement. I heard the metal sounds, and the ground sounds, and the throat sounds: they floated in on a gentle breeze of stench. Some hags were sweeping, some children brawling, some women popping bouillon cubes. Armageddon *bided* here. But I knew the horseman would come anyway.

I came into a valley where the dead lived. My mother approached me with welcoming arms. She did not speak, but implored me with her eyes. I spat in her face, and knew she was no one's mother. You would have done the same, *in my position.*

I will not always run. Sometime, the horse will tire.

# The Vain Vein

I AM a silver man. My muscles are dense with that metal, and my torso is sleek, and my brain is smooth. My human friends see themselves distorted in the curvatures of my body: they exclaim disgust, but secretly they are enraptured: they remain my friends. I have seen them in the distance see me: they do not realize I have seen them, for I am looking at my own body. They stop, and gaze at me for a while, and their eyes darken in that odd pupillary fashion. Their eyes become mineshafts in the sky, dank subterranean lengthy spaces floating *above* the terra in strong but frangible structures. O this perplexes me! If I were a finer metal, then perhaps my vision would be able to penetrate those black tunnels, which lead I am convinced into lit galleries hosting divine (yet solid) loci of volute definition. Strange brains that are not smooth. Thus, I feel, every so often, that I would like to be gold. But then, I should like to be platinum. But then, I should like to be philosophy. We metals shall never be satisfied. . . .

I keep my lodging at the Mercury River. There is an inn there, run by an iron woman. She is dull, and does not reflect; she is subject to corrosion. She *is* metal though, and I own the kinship. There are not many of us; we keep a solemn sodality, and accord every fellow metal being that dignity which befits even a base metal.

This is not to say that I do not accord my human friends respect. Do not misjudge me. It is simply that metallic nature is pure, whereas somatic nature is deceptive since it conceals its imperfections within a soft sort of orgasmic flesh. Yet it is this very softness which attracts me to my friends. I am unlike my metal brethren in this respect. Most metal men and women keep aloof from the fleshly genders: giving these reasons: obscenely fluid, lasciviously malleable, *perverse*.

(The iron woman brings me my meals. Otherwise, she leaves me alone. We do not speak usually, unless concerning the rent. She does not mention my human guests, although I know she is bothered by their coming; she cannot conceal the morose squeal her feet make on the steel steps as she guides visitors to my rooms.)

When my friends visit me, I do not speak much. They prattle on, as humans will, and I listen politely. They do not mind that my response is minimal. They understand my metal nature, at least insofar as it is resistive to conversation; for they do *not*, I assure you, *understand* my metal nature! They see my shiny surfaces, and *this* is what they understand. They see their own strange faces there, and *this* is what they understand. They see pupillary tunnels twisted by convexity, and *this* is what they understand.

I say, *this* is what they understand: I am them.

I know better, for I am me, but I feel no compulsion to correct their false notions. Their continual mistakes I find cute, their egocentric uncertainties endearing. They are so frail, so doomed.

Indeed, they bloom and wilt before my vision, these short-lived lifeforms: I have seen a hundred generations pass. They start rosy, but then a horrible jaundice creeps in, and afflicts not only their skins, but their bones as well. Gradually, yellow usurps; red yields, then flees. Yellow brings a brittleness into their human softness. There is a poignant crepitation whenever they reach or bend. Eventually, they crack apart, disintegrate into what they call *Death*, their slender bodies of latticeless chaos too fragile even to withstand the minuscule gravity of this planet. What little structure they possess dissolves, and without cohesion their constituent minerals are disseminated afar, so that a human man, *Dead*, may be a Mouth in Maui, a Nuque in Norway, an Organ in Ohio, and a Penis in Paraguay. It is almost absurd to assert their viability, since it is so temporary, but I assert it. My liberal ideas are not shared by many in the metal races.

I have two silver friends, though, who share my ideas. They visit me less often than do my human friends; and sometimes I even visit them, whereas I never visit humans. When they come, we bathe and frolic together in the river. It is such a pleasure to swim, and to admire the guttate bodies of my friends as they emerge from the quicksilver currents. Those quivering globules roll and mass together and give the illusion in our silver surfaces of an almost indecent liquescence. If a monk of the fundamentalist Fraternity of Lead were to see us, he would without doubt revile us for our obscene public display. The Mercury River is known for its decadence: which is why I choose to live there. My silver friends and I conduct orgies every so often, but in private: even we liberal silver men and women have our limits. I have many times remarked on the fundamental dichotomy of human sex and metal sex. Human sex entails a *casehardening* of male flesh, a *smelting* of female flesh: ductile extension, flexile intussusception: fusion, friction: *heat*: ecstasy occurs when the system melts. Metal sex is the precise opposite: it is a cyclical process of debasement and refinement: both bodies liquefy, alloy, together tainted anneal: reliquefy, rectify, anneal apart pure: this repeats, as many times as desired: ecstasy occurs in the *cool* periods of *mutual hardness*. My human friends wonder how *ecstasy* may result from such *stasis*; but I ask of them: does not the ecstasy of sex in both races arise from the unification of disparate entities? and therefore, if this union is the common and essential element, sex's universality, how may ecstasy in the midst of their *flux* be achieved? They cannot answer satisfactorily.

But O, I *would* like to know the answer. For it is indubitable that my human friends *do* achieve some sort of ecstasy in their strange comminglings, their oiled enlacements, their awkward flesh-meshes. I have theorized that they are seeking the same sort of experience—the *coolness*, the *mutual hardness*—but they are simply incapable by virtue of their fleshly nature. It is a paradox: for they are soft, yet cannot merge; whereas we are hard, yet may and *do* merge, to such a degree that individuality cannot be discerned but from within. I believe they envy me this: my hardness, my cold silver sheen. I have seen them looking. But I cannot know, can *never be certain*: for I cannot see *in*. I know the smooth brains of my silver friends, for we have been *mutually hard*. It is the human brain, however, which most piques my curiosity. But those tunnels are too dark, and I am not noble enough to shine *in*. I wish to enter *in*!

I met a gold man once. I would have asked him of the human mind. But he had no mouth, and he only nodded gravely when I introduced myself. I admired his bearing, his luster, his beauty. I would sacrifice my mouth to be a gold man.

# I Curse the Curs!

THERE is nothing I despise more than the curs. I would exterminate them all if I could. I would exterminate them *now*, and *permanently*. Why should I explain myself? It is obvious why the curs should be eliminated from our city. A dog should have a master. Without a master, a cur lives only for itself, is indiscriminate in every unclean dominion, snuffles among the horrors of humanity's very *bowels*, and spreads disease from one section of the city to the next. A master cares for his cur, delivers it to the veterinarian for the appropriate vaccinations, feeds it, grooms it, and keeps it clean.

I have walked these streets plenty enough. I have seen the curs loping about, sickening blotched tongues dangling wetly down—practically slurping up the sludge from the dirty pavement! The much-trod carpets of their mangy backs look to be infested with God-knows-what manner of insectile life—larvae, lice, ticks. . . . *I shudder in the imagining.*

Look on that cur there. He lacks a history—has no master. I cannot ask his master, "Where has your dog been?" I cannot know how that nostril was mutilated. The foreshortened tail, the strange burrs in its paws, the missing ear, the bedraggled lips drooping down past its jaw revealing blacktar gums: how did these come about?—any number of disgusting *images* arises before my appalled consciousness. The cur whines as its wagging picks up and its snout burrows deeper into the pile it has been sniffing. It has found a rotten fruit. The cur gobbles greedily what any well-heeled dog would leave to the floor. Indeed, the cur searches desperately for more. It paces the wall alongside which stretches the spilled trash (which spillage I am certain the cur abetted), and pokes its nose in with infinite hope, and blows and sneezes according with the odd powders and chemicals to be found deep midst the spreading detritus. The cur leaves, having exhausted the possibilities, yet *stays*, in spirit, for the trash is still there against that wall, even dispersing down the street, even insinuating itself into every crevice of the city, thankful to its *cur*-progenitor, without which it would have been hauled away to some far site to be compacted and buried away from sight.

And most distressingly, there is the problem of the bad example these curs set for the youth of our city. The curs have no decency, no code of conduct. They defecate in the gutter, piss on the flagpoles, and, most abominably, *rut where they please*. Just the other day, I came upon some children giggling in an alleyway as they observed the curs propagating with exertion upon each other's backs. Let me reassure you, I shooed the children away, telling them, "Do not do as the curs do!" and then *I took care of those curs.*

# Bone Hotel

A GATHERING commenced in my hometown. From all the reaches of the world it seemed came riches to my town, to celebrate some historical event. I watched their gleamy limousines arrive into and leave the circle drive of the hotel. Emergent from the black cars were wizened bejeweled men bent and cracked with so much age in them I could not stand to look. But I looked! I could *not* refrain, *O could not!*

They hobbled into the lobby and waited patiently for service. The bellhop fainted from fright. I was enlisted to carry their bags and cases up to their specially appointed rooms. I looked into the eyes of him as he doled out my tip. His eyes were generous, his tip was not. I could not reconcile this paradox, but I had work to do. I delivered each rich man to his reserved suite, and each was unstinting in his gaze, but stinted in the tip. I could hardly object: *I was not a bellhop.*

The last rich man to arrive was no man. She was beautiful, and I was in love with her even when I could see no more of her than her single emergent leg. Her eyes found me immediately, even though she could not have known me for the bellhop, since I had not donned the uniform (it did not fit). She smiled, and took me captive, and gestured to her trunks which were strapped to the roof, being so large. I took them down with help from her chauffeur, and together we hauled them up ten flights of stairs (she insisted on stairs) to the penthouse suite, which was the most luxuriant suite in the hotel. Her chauffeur departed, and she called my attention to her gaze. I nodded, mute. There was no tip.

I saw her almost constantly during the festivities. She presided over the events, for she was a personage of no small eminence in our country. Every now and then, as her gaze swept over the crowds from her high ceremonial throne, I thought I detected a hesitation in her eyes, as if searching something out. I believed it was me she was searching for. I did not present myself to her gaze, although I yearned to do so.

The final night of the gathering, I hid myself in one of her trunks. When she arrived back into her room later, I listened as her servants prepared her for her sleep. When they tiptoed out of the room, I heard the restless rustle of her sheets. I fell fast asleep to the sounds of her bedtime pleasure.

I awoke at the limousine's ignition. The trip lasted fifteen hours. Eventually, doors slammed, trunks thumped the ground, and I in my trunk was lifted and dropped. I heard her voice. She ordered her footmen to carry all the trunks to the Bone Room. I shivered when I heard. After being carried up many flights of stairs, my trunk was dropped, and unlatched. After I was certain the footmen had left the room, I emerged cautiously from my hiding place. Blinking, I saw nine boys standing in nine open trunks, their backs hunched in pain postures. A tenth trunk was still shut. After a few minutes, the lid eased upward and a boy stood stretching his arms till his bones crackled. This incited me to stretch in a similar fashion, and it was the sweetest agony I had ever known. All the boys stretched their bones now, and the sound of crackling filled the room.

We said nothing to each other, and a few hours later, eleven footmen entered and guided us to our specially appointed suites. There were mirrors in my suite, and I gazed for hours into my wizened eyes. They were not generous, but there is time yet.

# A Universal Sensation

THE way she looked at me, I experienced a universal sensation, one, by definition, not unfamiliar to you and therefore unnecessary of elaboration. (The limpid pools, the shimmer of love, the moonlit porches, etc.) She purposely dropped her handbag (just before the bus arrived), its contents spilling across the sidewalk, and the way she crouched to gather up her things served not only to display advantageously the shadowed foyer of her thigh-length skirt, but by its coquettish angle (with respect to me) to invite my assistance. It required the calculation of my year's remaining sick leave for me to reach the conclusion that possibilities existed. (I am a dedicated professional. The allures of love are insufficient to compensate me for the loss of my source of income, and thus, even in a love story such as this one, I, the protagonist, would not dream of jeopardizing my "Bank Of Hours." How these bohemians with their "Free Spirits" manage to undertake the slog of Life without address to pecuniary considerations never ceases to amaze and dispirit me.)

"The bus!" she shrieked, then giggled, once we'd finished refilling her handbag. "They've abandoned us." I concurred, noting the gorgeous line of her cheek, the escaped strands of her tied-back hairstyle waving alluringly in the soft breeze, the slender neck so precisely adapted, topologically, to kisses. I suggested we share a coffee while we waited for the next bus. And she was all for it, complete with smiling blushes, batting eyelashes, and the brief, conspiratorial press of fingertips against my forearm as she intensely held my gaze. (In such moments, it is true, the woman is the Master; it is only later that the man comes into his dominating role. His primary duty, initially, is only to appreciate (and remark upon) the charm and beauty of his feminine interlocutor.)

She sipped at her *café au lait*. I admired the plumping of her lips at the rim of her bowl-shaped cup. The server, in deference to the austere pose of our mutual and exclusive regard across that small circle of table, hesitated to interrupt us with his inquiry of satisfaction. We delved deeply into our attraction, even as we stayed carefully at surface in conversation. Chatting, we tastefully avoided subjects that might lead to contention. (Politics, philosophy, gender studies, etc.) The weather and the sports teams were sufficient to our purposes. With a wink, I mentioned that while caffeine was most stimulative as a morning beverage, alcohol's utility might be employed at any wakeful hour. That was when she coyly invited me back to her place for stronger drinks (and implied bouts of passion). I consented and thoroughly enjoyed my day with her. Before I departed, I slaughtered her so as to fix the incident in my memory (and also to eliminate all evidence of duplicity toward my employer in claiming to be sick when I was, in fact, perfectly healthy).

# The Pain Painter

NOT long ago, a man came to me with a photo of his happy wife. He asked me what I could do. I examined the photo, and was intrigued by the faint lubricious luster in the wife's eyes. I consented to paint him. He sat for me every day. Green dominated this piece. Sharp angles. I kept the photo for reference, returning it only when the painting was finished. The man was pleased with the result. He invited me to dinner not long afterward. He proudly pointed to the painting above his mantel. It was red now. His wife prepared our meal. The meat was raw, and seasoned with mown grass. The man wolfed it down with relish, and demanded a second serving. I concentrated on the side dishes. When the meal was finished, the man instructed his wife to lie on the cleared table and raise her skirt. He told me this was dessert. I glanced at the painting. There were small green circles within the greater red. When I looked back, I saw that the wife's pussy was zippered shut, and padlocked. The man told me this was for *security reasons*. He showed me the key he kept on a chain around his neck. He unlocked the pussy, and unzipped it. The wife emitted a shriek, and the man shuddered with repressed ecstasy at the sound. He unzipped his pants and hefted his member out. He caressed the zipper (of the pussy) with the member, and the member grew. In forceful quick repetitions he plunged her pussy as he would a clogged toilet, without relent until the waters gurgled and the pipes flowed clear. I declined dessert. The man seemed disappointed, but shrugged and zipped the wife back up. When the padlock was *secure*, the wife stood and arranged her skirt, then went to do the dishes. The man thanked me once again for the painting, which I noticed now was blue. I wish, *just once*, a client's painting would remain faithful to *my* vision.

Soon, as I had somewhat expected, the wife came to me with a commission. She showed me a photo of her happy husband. I consented to paint her. She sat for me every day. Volume dominated this piece. Complex curves. The woman was pleased with the result. She invited me to dinner not long afterward. The husband was not to be seen all evening. The woman and I ate an elegant meal of *escargots* from the same plate. In the candlelight, her pale skin seemed to glow. I told her she appeared happy. She laughed, and nodded. I asked her where she kept her painting. (I had noticed earlier that the husband's painting no longer hung over the mantel.) She told me it was too beautiful for public display, so she kept it in her closet, for *private viewing*. She told me that since I was the painter, however, I could see it. She led me upstairs and through her bedroom to the closet. It was the walk-in kind, so I walked in, and flipped the light-switch. The husband was here, standing against the back wall, nude. He held the painting, and his face strove to be impassive, but I detected fatigue in his taut cheeks. I noticed that the composition was much simpler, and the colors more vivid. There was a great deal of flatness in the painting. The woman attempted to seduce me, but I declined, telling her I was homosexual. I was not, but it was an incontrovertible excuse.

# In That Country

I LIVED in that country where infibulation of the daughters is custom, and my terror drove me into flight. It took me five hours over rocky terrain to traverse the ten miles between my village and the border. The patrols missed me, for it was the dead of night, and I was small (only seven years old), blending in with the flora whenever I heard the tramp of the boots. Soon, I was in another country. I could hardly believe it: there seemed no difference! The plants were the same as those I knew, the dirt flattened in the same manner beneath my feet, the wind reached in under my skirt and cooled me in my crevices, and *O, I knew the difference!*

I succumbed soon to exhaustion. I knew it would not be wise to fall asleep in the road, so I curled up beneath a bush some ways *off to the side.* When I awoke, there was a boy sitting on top of me. He wore no pants, and his scepter was raised diagonally with my throat. He sawed it back and forth in a slow rhythm under my chin. I did not struggle, for he was older than I, and his hands could strangle me in mere seconds. The boy continued with his strange motion for a long time. His eyes were shut. He did not know I had awakened. I lowered my chin to pin his scepter to my clavicle. He cried out, and my torso was suddenly hot with some strange fluid. I thought it was my blood. I screamed, *You are the Angel of Death!* The boy shrieked. Tears of terror sprang out of his eyes. He ran off, leaving his pants behind. Since I was naked, and could not find my clothes, I wore the pants. I used leaves to clean my breast.

I was very hungry. I ate some of the leaves, but disgorged them violently. I followed the road, staying *off to the side*. Cars passed every now and then, eructant and ancient: I hid whenever I heard the distant belches. My chest and back grew hot to the touch as a result of the o'erlooming sun. I was very thirsty, whereas my hunger waned. I have never been able to eat at midday. I found a puddle, and slaked my thirst at it. I retched violently, and regretted the puddle. When I came upon another puddle, I declined its cool invitation. Instead, I removed my pants, and sat in the puddle, so that my legs were submerged, and my belly. All that could be seen of me were my breast and arms and head. I splashed happily in the puddle for quite some time.

My joy drew the attention of a cur. He stood at the edge of the puddle, wagging his tail and nodding as he panted. His eyes were gentle, I thought, they examined me gently. I giggled, loving the cur, *the cur's gentle eyes*, and stood, stepped out of the puddle to pet him. He drew his pink tongue in and snapped his jaws, grunting. He sniffed my folds and crevices, and lapped inside with his flexible tongue. I was too surprised to reprimand him. He knocked me over, being a large cur, and mounted me, taking my virginity as I screamed and wriggled. The cur was too heavy, I could not escape him. I was forced to endure his cock for an hour. He could not withdraw until his ecstasy was done. When he trotted off, I lay still for a while, gathering strength, then bathed in the puddle, cleaned his spunk out of me. I wished to cry, but did not, for *I did not wish to cry.*

I thought, *Now no man will ever corrupt me. The cur has done me a service.*

Clothed in my pants, I strode confidently down the road. Two cars passed by without even slowing. A third squealed as it stopped, and a thin man leaned out of the passenger window. He asked me if I needed assistance. I told him food and some clothing would be appreciated. He nodded pleasantly, and gestured for me to crawl in through the window. I examined the car, and adjudged it disreputable, but the promise finally of an assuagement to my raging hunger compelled me to shake off my doubt and assent to the thin man's proposal. He held me in his lap, and caressed my thighs. The woman driving paid no attention. She wore sunglasses, so that I could not see her eyes, and this was fortunate, for *I did not wish to see her eyes.* The thin man's fingers unbuttoned my pants, and slid through my folds, and entered my crevices. I squirmed and shuddered, but did not prevent him. *I could not have prevented him.* The drive lasted hours, and the thin man's fingers never tired. *I* tired. I fell asleep, even while the thin man's fingers were entrenched deep in my body.

This was my dream: God placed a diamond in my mouth, and commanded me, *Never swallow this.* Then he sewed my lips together.

I woke to find myself in a diner. I was dressed in a pretty pink frock, trimmed with lace and soft against my skin. The woman sat across from me. The thin man was not here. The woman ate her meal in silence, and I ate mine. She still wore her sunglasses, and I was glad. Her lips and cheeks were delicate and smooth, yet her forehead was pitted and scarred in so many layers that a road for tractors would have seemed less rough. When we were finished eating, she stood and walked away with the bill. I followed, not knowing what to do. The woman paid, and we left. I sat in the passenger seat, and wondered where the thin man had gone. We had travelled many miles before I chanced to peek into the back seat. His head sat there, secured with a seatbelt. His hand rested next to it. I wondered where the remainder of his body was. I did not dare ask the woman. *She would not have answered.* I felt terror as the car hurtled relentlessly forward. I felt the thin man's eyes on me, leering over the seatbelt. *He was not alive, yet his gaze was on me.* Terror roamed my body, lingered in my folds and crevices. The car hurtled relentlessly forward. Terror took the thin man's gaze and scrubbed my skin as with a soapy loofah, cleansing deep into every pore. The car hurtled relentlessly forward. The woman driving wore dark sunglasses. I sat without motion, and terror exhausted my body.

I thought, *No man will ever corrupt me. But what of the Bitch and the Dead?*

We drove into a city. I adjudged it disreputable. The woman parked the car in an empty garage. The slam of the doors echoed for an entire minute. The woman had the thin man's head under her arm, and his hand was in her pocket. She took my hand in hers, and led me to an elevator. We ascended for an entire minute. Her hand

was cold and dry. It gripped my bones with ancient con-
fidence. *I was not confident.* The elevator opened directly
on her apartment. She took me in, released my hand.
She set the head on the TV, and behind it with a ham-
mer nailed the hand to the wall, palm facing out. She
fixed a meal for us, and we ate in silence. She still wore
her sunglasses, and I was glad. The woman washed the
dishes when we were through, and went to bed. I was left
to my own devices. I examined myself in the bathroom
mirror, admired the pretty frock. I played games in the
sink with the running water. I filled the tub and took a
bath. I am splashing happily in the bath now. My joy has
drawn the woman's attention, aroused her from her bed.
She is standing beside the tub, nodding as she pants. She
holds a flint knife in her hand. The woman removes her
sunglasses, and her eyes are mad.

# What Breathes Down There?

AND how many times have I looked into that sewer, wondering, *What breathes down there?* O, I have lived in this apartment so long.

*Something is breathing.* That is the thought I wake with.

(The morning comes, and absolves me of sleep, and the wind wakes the streets, and I hear the sirens, and in the walls the molecules sleep, and what will come to absolve them of sleep?)

I stand at my window. I see the street below. There are nostrils in the street. The street is not solid. The hollow street conducts more than the traffic of men and curs: *something is breathing*, and it is below the street. *What breathes down there?*

I stand on a floor. She is not far from me. I can smell her musk even here. She is sweet. I tremble already, in my mind. In my mind, my nose is in her cunt. She is sweet, in my mind. In my mind, she trembles already.

I hold a newspaper. Her musk is in my blood now. *She is sweet.* She stands not two feet from me! I could touch her, in my mind. In my mind, I could love her.

I lean against a railing. She is just over there. She feeds

the llama. Even more powerful than the llama's stench is her musk. Her musk is in my brain. I drink from her armpit, in my mind. In my mind, she is sweet. I love her for herself, in my mind. In my mind, I love her for myself.

And it comes to me: *She is walking on breath.*

And how many times have I looked into that sewer, wondering, *What breathes down there?*

She stands on a floor. I am far from her, but I can see her. I can smell her musk, in my mind. In my mind, she is sweet.

She holds a newspaper. I could touch her, in my mind. In my mind, I hold a newspaper. She could touch me, in my mind. In my mind, she holds a newspaper.

She leans against a railing. I am ten miles away, but *she is sweet.*

And it comes to me: *She is walking on breath.*

And how many times have I looked into that sewer, wondering, *What breathes down there?* O, I have lived in this apartment so long.

*Something is breathing.* I eat with that thought in my mind.

*41*

The dishes are dirty. They stink in the sink. I leave them to stink, and stand by the window. I look into the street, and *something is breathing.*

I turn from the window, gasping for breath. I sink into my cushions.

(In the sink, the dishes stink.)

From nostrils in the street rise its exhalations. Its inhalations are not to be seen. I am in my cushions, and yet I wonder, *What breathes down there?*

Her lover wraps her in his arm. They are just over there, admiring the fountain. He can smell her musk, in my mind. In my mind, I can smell her musk. She is wrapped in my arm, in my mind. In my mind, she is sweet.

Her lover presents his shoulder to her cheek. She rests against him, in the breeze. In the breeze, I can smell her musk.

Her lover carries her to the fountain. She kicks and giggles like a little girl. In my mind, she is a little girl. I can smell her musk, in my mind. In my mind, my nose is in her cunt. She kicks and giggles, in my mind.

And it comes to me: *They are walking on breath.*

And how many times have I looked into that sewer, wondering, *What breathes down there?*

She wraps her lover in her arm. They are among the high buildings, and the insolent crowds. I can smell her musk even here. Her musk wipes away the crowds, in my mind. In my mind, she is sweet. *She is sweet*, in my mind. In my mind, her musk wipes away her lover.

She presents her breasts to her lover's cheek. He listens to her heart, and chants its rhythm back to her. In my mind, her heart beats.

She leads her lover to the shade of a tree. The sky grows grey, and the shade disappears. In my mind, the sky grows grey. The shade disappears, in my mind. Her lover looks at her solemnly. She looks at her lover solemnly back. Solemnity shades them, in my mind. In my mind, *she is sweet*.

And it comes to me: *They are walking on breath.*

And how many times have I looked into that sewer, wondering, *What breathes down there?* O, I have lived in this apartment so long!

*Something is breathing.* That is my thought as I grip my cock.

(The agony comes, and absolves me of joy, and the sun lights the street, and the voices are winging over the buildings, and joy moves the molecules in their sleep, and what will come to absolve them of joy?)

I kneel at my window. My palms are pressed for the street below. *Something is breathing,* and it is below the street. Its exhalations rise from nostrils in the street. The hollow street conducts immane inhalations. I speak to the sewer, saying, *What breathes down there?*

And it comes to me: *I am walking on breath.*

And how many times have I looked into that sewer, wondering, *What breathes down there?*

As many times as I have been answered: *I am the city. You are my breath.*

www.ingramcontent.com/pod-product-compliance
Lightning Source LLC
Chambersburg PA
CBHW032045180726
48284CB00008B/2763